~ The St. Patrick's Day Shillelagh ~

DAY AFTER DAY, Fergus felt a rumble in his empty belly as he sat beside his favorite blackthorn tree, watching the clouds reach down from the sky and touch the earth.

It was a terrible time in Ireland, when Fergus was a child. The potatoes had rotted in the fields and children lay in their beds at night hungry.

Late one night, when the peat fire had burned low, Fergus woke to the sound of his parents' worried whispers. When the sun rose through the mist of dawn, they told him to say farewell to Ireland.

They were sailing to America.

On his last night in his homeland, when the stars were shining their very brightest and the moonlight shimmered on the land, Fergus crept from his window and cut a branch from the blackthorn tree. He would take a piece of Ireland with him on his journey across the ocean.

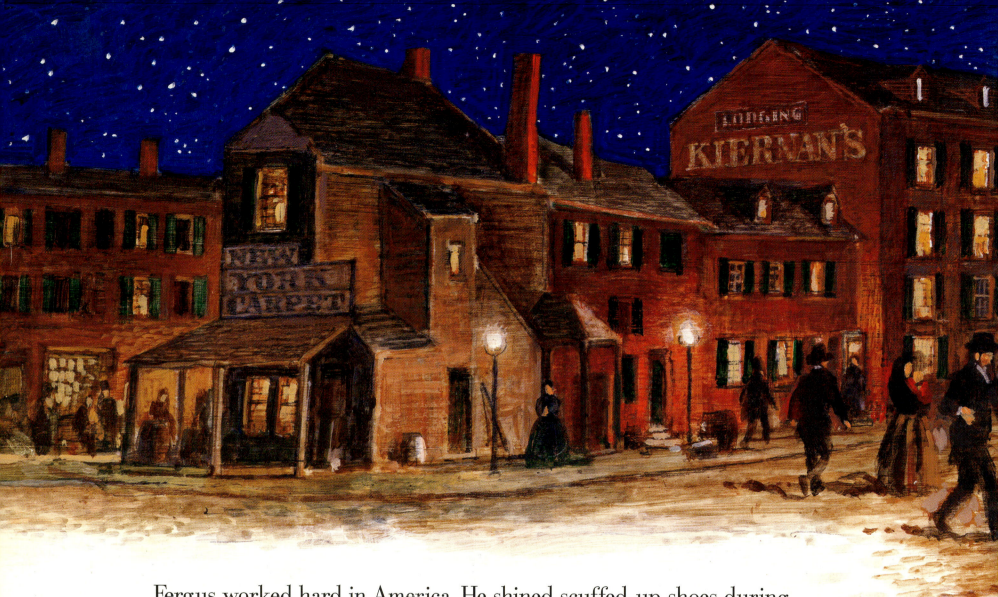

Fergus worked hard in America. He shined scuffed-up shoes during
the day, and for a few pennies more, sold newspapers at night. These were
difficult jobs for a skinny boy with tired legs.

When he grew to be a man, he laid the tracks where the trains now run.

On Sundays, wearing his finest suit and carrying his shillelagh,
Fergus courted the lovely lass who came to be his bride.

Fergus never learned to read and he never learned to write, but
he always had a tale to tell. On St. Patrick's Day of every year, he
told the story of the terrible hunger and his journey to America.

One year, Fergus placed the shillelagh in his son Declan's hands
and said, "Take this branch as a memory of Ireland."

And so it was Declan's turn to tell the shillelagh story on St. Patrick's
Day.

Declan rose before dawn every day. He labored in sun and rain, cold and heat, high above the East River, building the Brooklyn Bridge. His legs grew strong, his hands blistered and rough.

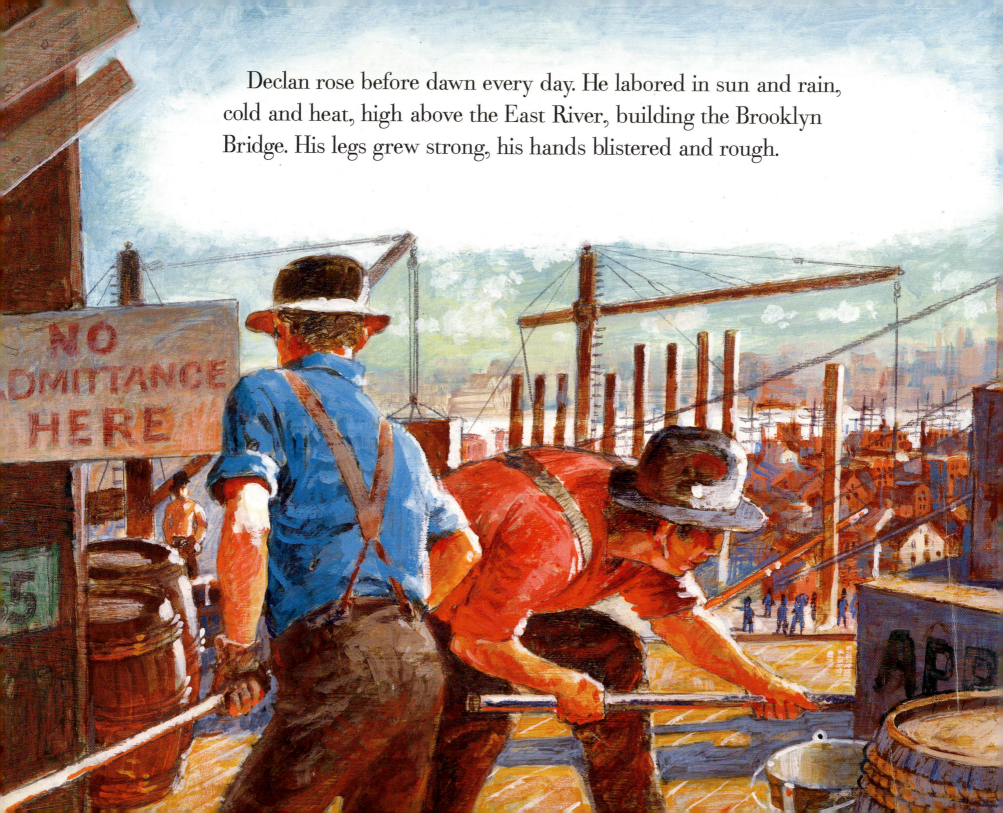

Declan always had a joke to share and a kind word for anyone passing on the street. And at the end of the day, he had a gentle hug for his wee son, Emmet.

On St. Patrick's Day, when the stars were shining and the bonfires had burned low, Declan told the story of Fergus and his shillelagh to all who gathered near. When Emmet grew to be a man, Declan placed the shillelagh in his hands. "The past that walks with me today will walk with you tomorrow," he told his son.

Everyone in the neighborhood knew Emmet and his grand singing voice. On St. Patrick's Day, it was Emmet singing Gaelic songs that made the grownups laugh and dance and cry.

Year after year, Emmet told the shillelagh story until the year he left to fight in World War I. While he was away at war, the story was not told.

When Emmet returned with an injured leg, it was the shillelagh he leaned on to help him walk.

When Emmet's leg healed, he placed the shillelagh in the hands of his daughter, Mary Maeve, and told her, "Remember, a good story takes its time in the making and its time in the telling."

Mary Maeve was a green-eyed lass who loved to dance a reel—toes pointed, hair flying as she leaped to an Irish tune. When young men left to fight in World War II, Mary Maeve and other women took their places in the factories. For weeks—then months, then years, Mary Maeve drilled hole after hole into the silver metal of airplanes.

One St. Patrick's Day, Mary Maeve placed the shillelagh in the hands of her son, Garrett. "May the stories of our past guide you to your future," she told him.

Garrett was a big, tall man with bushy eyebrows and eyes that twinkled even when his face was still. He became a music teacher, helping children to play tin whistle, fiddle, flute, and drum. One, two, three, four—he tapped out the rhythm with his shillelagh.

Garrett was not a man who easily cried, but on the day his son Ryan graduated from college, tears of pride welled in his eyes.

And so the shillelagh was passed down through the generations. From Fergus to Declan, Declan to Emmet, Emmet to Mary Maeve, and Mary Maeve to Garrett, who gave the shillelagh to Ryan. Then Ryan moved to a new house and put the shillelagh in a closet.

There it stayed until years later when Ryan's daughter, Kayleigh, found the dusty shillelagh while playing hide-and-seek.

"What's this?" Kayleigh asked her father.

"A story I forgot to tell," said Ryan. He put down the cooking pot and turned toward his daughter.

"This shillelagh is our past," he said. "Its story has been told on St. Patrick's Day for many years, through many generations."

"Why didn't you tell the story to me?" Kayleigh asked him. "I would have listened."

"I got so busy worrying about tomorrow I forgot to tell you our family's story of yesterday. On St. Patrick's Day, your Grandpa Garrett would love to tell you the shillelagh story."

And so on St. Patrick's Day, when the stars were shining their very brightest and the moon glowed, Kayleigh sat down beside her Grandpa Garrett.

"Long ago and far away," he began, "in a land where clouds come down from the sky and touch the earth, in a country that is every color of green, lived a lad who answered to the name of Fergus. When the hunger of the potato famine forced his family to leave the land he loved, Fergus cut a branch from his favorite blackthorn tree and whittled it into a fine shillelagh. Fergus brought a piece of Ireland with him to America."

When Grandpa Garrett finished talking, he placed the shillelagh in Kayleigh's hands and said, "A good story never has to end as long as someone remembers to keep telling it." And so it was Kayleigh's turn to tell the tale of her family and their shillelagh.

"Now," said Grandpa Garrett, "I'd be honored to have a dance with my little lass, Kayleigh."

With the shillelagh held between their hands, Kayleigh and her Grandpa Garrett danced, on St. Patrick's Day, by the light of the stars and the glow of the moon.

To Tom and Megan: May your lives be filled with stories. — J. N.

This book is dedicated to my immigrant forebears, who had the courage, vision,
and strength to succeed in creating a new life in a challenging land. — B. F. S.

~ About the Potato Famine ~

In 1845, the potato was the main source of food in rural Ireland. When a fungus rotted the potatoes, many went hungry. Between 1845 and 1851, an estimated one million people died of starvation. During the same time, another million emigrated to America.

Those who survived the difficult journey across the Atlantic Ocean began new lives in the United States, helping to shape American society.

Library of Congress Cataloging-in-Publication Data

Nolan, Janet.
The St. Patrick's Day shillelagh / by Janet Nolan ; illustrated by Ben F. Stahl.
p. cm.
Summary: On his way from Ireland to America to escape the potato famine, young Fergus carves a shillelagh from his favorite blackthorn tree, and each St. Patrick's Day for generations, his story is retold by one of his descendants.
ISBN 0-8075-7344-2 (hardcover)
[1. Irish Americans — Fiction. 2. Storytelling — Fiction. 3. Saint Patrick's Day — Fiction.
4. Emigration and immigration — Fiction. 5. Ireland — History — Famine, 1845-1852 — Fiction.] I. Stahl, Ben F.,
ill. II. Title. PZ7.N6785 St 2002 [Fic] — dc21 2002001953

The design is by Scott Piehl.
The paintings for this book were extensively researched in New York City.
They were done in acrylic on gesso board.

For more information about Albert Whitman & Company,
visit our web site at www.albertwhitman.com